JACK AND THE BEANSTALK

SIMON AND SCHUSTER BOOKS FOR YOUNG READERS
Simon & Schuster Building,
Rockefeller Center,
1230 Avenue of the Americas,
New York, New York 10020.
Text copyright © 1989 by Susan Pearson
Illustrations copyright © 1989 by James Warhola

SIMON AND SCHUSTER BOOKS FOR YOUNG READERS
is a trademark of Simon & Schuster Inc.

Manufactured in the United States of America

10 9 8 7 6 5 4 3 2 1

Library of Congress Cataloging-in-Publication Data
Pearson, Susan.
Jack and the beanstalk.
Summary: A boy climbs to the top of a giant beanstalk where he
uses his quick wits to outsmart a giant and make his and his
mother's fortune.
[1. Fairy tales. 2. Folklore—England. 3. Giants—Folklore.]
I. Warhola, James, ill. II. Jack and the beanstalk. III. Title.
PZ8.P288Jac 1989   88-19793
ISBN 0-671-67196-0

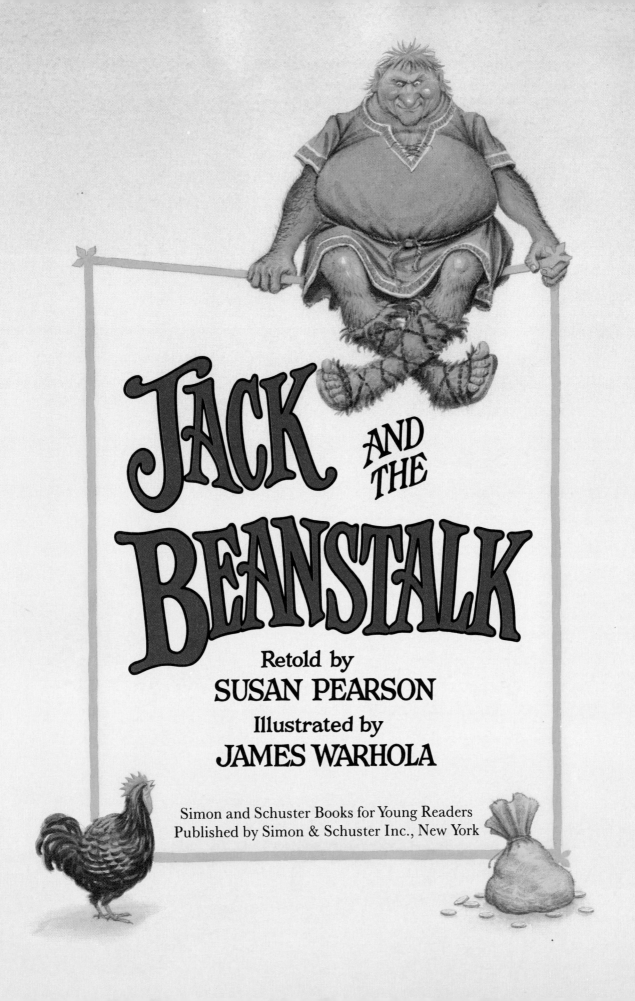

JACK AND THE BEANSTALK

Retold by
SUSAN PEARSON

Illustrated by
JAMES WARHOLA

Simon and Schuster Books for Young Readers
Published by Simon & Schuster Inc., New York

For Pam Pollack
—SP

To Tyson, Pablo, Zonker, Babe, and Pop
—JW

ONCE UPON A TIME, a widow lived in the country with her only son, named Jack, and their cow, named Milky-White. They were very poor. All they had to live on was the milk the cow gave, which Jack took to market and sold.

But one morning Milky-White gave no milk.

"Oh, what shall we do?" cried the widow, wringing her hands.

"Cheer up, Mother," said Jack. "I'll take Milky-White to market and sell her."

And he took the cow by her halter and started off.

"Remember, Jack, she's all we have," his mother called after him. "Be sure you get a good price for her."

Jack hadn't gone far when he met a funny-looking old man.

"Good morning, Jack," said the old man. "And where are you off to in such a hurry?"

"Good morning to you, sir," said Jack, wondering how the old man knew his name. "I'm on my way to market to sell Milky-White."

At that the old man began to laugh. "That's a tall job for a short fellow," he said. "Why, I'll bet you don't even know how many beans make five."

"Two in each hand and one in my mouth," said Jack, sharp as a needle.

"Right you are," said the old man, and he reached into his pocket and pulled out five beans. "Since you're so smart, I'll make you a deal. You give me Milky-White, and I'll give you these."

"What!" cried Jack. "My beautiful cow for five ordinary beans?"

"Not ordinary beans," said the old man. He held out his hand. "These are magic beans, Jack. Plant them in the ground tonight, and by morning they'll have grown right up to the sky."

"Right up to the sky?" asked Jack, amazed.

"You have my word on it," said the old man. "If they don't, you can have your cow back again."

"Well…" said Jack.

The old man closed his hand around the beans. "Perhaps you're not the smart boy I took you for," he said. "Well, it's no matter." He put his hand back into his pocket.

"No, wait!" cried Jack. "I'll do it!"

And quick as a wink, the swap was made.

When Jack got home, his mother was waiting for him.

"Back already?" she said. "You must have found an eager buyer! How much did you get?"

"You'll never guess, Mother," said Jack.

"Five pounds…ten pounds…fifteen…twenty?"

"I knew you'd never guess," said Jack. "Look!" He held out his hand. "We'll plant these in the ground tonight, and in the morning…"

"Beans!" cried his mother. "Five moldy beans for our good cow? Oh, Jack, you've been swindled. What good are beans we can't even eat?" And she snatched them from Jack's hand and threw them out the window. All this made Jack feel so miserable that he went straight to bed without his supper.

The next morning when Jack woke up, his room looked very odd. Instead of sunlight streaming in, strange shadows darted about the walls. Jack jumped out of bed and ran to the window. There outside was a giant beanstalk. So the old man had told the truth after all!

Jack pulled on his clothes and ran outside. Up, up, up the beanstalk grew, through the clouds, like a ladder to the sky. Jack wondered what magic might be at the top. There was only one way to find out. Jack began to climb.

Up he went, above his cottage, above the treetops, until they seemed just tiny specks beneath him. Soon he could see the whole countryside for miles around, but still he climbed. Right through the clouds, until at last he reached the top. A long road stretched before him into the distance. There was nothing to do but to follow the road. On and on and on he walked, until he reached a great tall house. By then Jack was feeling very hungry, having climbed and walked all that way with no supper the night before and no breakfast that morning. He was happy to see a great tall woman standing on the doorstep stirring something in a great black pot.

"Good morning, ma'am," said Jack. "Do you think you could give me some breakfast, please?"

"Breakfast!" cried the great tall woman. "If it's breakfast you want, it's breakfast you'll be! My husband is an Ogre, and there's nothing he likes better than grilled boy on toast. You'd better be off before he comes home."

"Oh, please, ma'am," begged Jack, "give me something to eat first. I've had nothing since yesterday morning, and I may as well be grilled as die of hunger."

So the Ogre's wife, who was not altogether bad, took Jack into the kitchen and gave him some bread and milk.

But Jack had just begun to eat when—thump THUMP THUMP—the whole house began to shake. The Ogre was coming!

"Oh, dear," said the Ogre's wife, "whatever shall I do with you? Quick now! Hide in here!" And she pushed Jack into her huge oven just in time.

Jack peeked through a crack beside the oven door. The Ogre was enormous! Three sheep were tied to his belt, and he carried a club the size of a small tree. Pausing in the doorway, he sniffed the air. "What's this I smell?" he asked, then began to prowl around the kitchen, muttering to himself,

"Fee-fi-fo-fum!
I smell the blood of an Englishman.
Be he live or be he dead,
I'll grind his bones to make my bread."

"Nonsense, dear," said his wife. "You smell the bones of that boy you had for supper yesterday. I'm boiling them down for soup. Now give me those sheep so I can get dinner started while you eat your breakfast."

So the Ogre sat down to a breakfast of five meat pies, three roast turkeys, ten pounds of fried potatoes, eight dozen eggs, and a few gallons of hot chocolate.

When he had finished eating, he fetched three bags of gold pieces from a big chest and sat down again to count them. All that warm milk must have caught up with him, though, for soon his head was nodding and not long after he was fast asleep.

When the Ogre's snores sounded like a summer thunderstorm, Jack knew it was safe to come out of the oven. The Ogre's wife was in the pantry. Jack tiptoed past the Ogre, snatched up one of the bags of gold, and ran off with it over his shoulder.

When he reached the beanstalk, he threw the bag down into his own backyard, then climbed down after it.

Jack and his mother lived well for some time on the bag of gold. But at last they came to the end of it, and Jack made up his mind to try his luck once more.

One fine morning he got up early and climbed up through the clouds to the top of the beanstalk as he had done before. Then he followed the road to the great tall house, and there, sure enough, standing on the door-step, was the great tall woman.

"Good morning, ma'am," said Jack. "Do you think you could give me some breakfast, please?"

"Go away," said the Ogre's wife crossly. "The last time I gave a boy some breakfast, he made off with a bag of gold. Why, you might be that very one. You boys all look the same to me."

"I believe I heard about that boy," said Jack. "I'd tell you if I weren't too hungry to say another word."

The Ogre's wife was so curious that she took Jack into the kitchen and fed him; but before she had a chance to ask for his story—thump THUMP THUMP—the Ogre came home. Again she pushed Jack into the oven.

This time the Ogre carried three calves on his belt. He tossed them on the counter. "For dinner," he grumbled. "I haven't caught a boy in days." Suddenly, he threw his head back and sniffed. "But what's that I smell?" he asked. "Wife, you must have found me a boy for breakfast!"

"Wishful thinking," said the wife. "There's no boy in here."

But the Ogre prowled around the kitchen just the same, muttering,

> "Fee-fi-fo-fum!
> I smell the blood of an Englishman.
> Be he live or be he dead,
> I'll grind his bones to make my bread."

At last he gave up and sat down to a breakfast of sixteen melons, two roast pigs, three gallons of oatmeal, fifteen mince pies, and hot chocolate.

When he had finished, he called out, "Wife, bring me my magic hen!"

So the Ogre's wife brought in a small black hen, which she placed on the table in front of the Ogre. Then she went outside to hang the wash.

"Lay!" the Ogre commanded the hen, and at once it laid a golden egg. "Lay!" he said again, and there was another beautiful, shining, golden egg. The Ogre amused himself in this way for some time, but finally his head began to nod.

When his snores sounded like the ocean beating against a rocky shore, Jack knew it was safe to leave the oven. Carefully, he tiptoed over to the hen, caught it by the leg, and was off. But just as he was going out the door, the hen gave a cackle, which woke the Ogre.

"Wife!" Jack heard him roar. "What have you done with my magic hen?" But that was all Jack heard, for he was running like lightning for the beanstalk.

Down he climbed, faster than a falling bean, to show his mother the magic hen.

"Lay, please," he told it. And sure enough it laid a golden egg every time Jack asked.

For some time Jack and his mother lived very comfortably on the golden eggs laid by the magic hen. But then one day the hen stopped laying.

"What could be wrong with her?" Jack's mother wondered.

"There's only one way to find out," said Jack, and back up the beanstalk he went.

This time he knew better than to ask for breakfast. Instead he hid in the bushes until the Ogre's wife came out to fetch some water. Then he slipped into the kitchen and hid inside a copper pot. He hadn't been there long when—thump THUMP THUMP—he heard the Ogre coming.

Jack peeked out from beneath the lid. This time the Ogre carried three fat oxen. He had barely tossed them on the counter when he began to shout, "I smell him, wife, I smell him! I know there's a boy here somewhere!"

"Well, if there is," said his wife, "you can be sure it's that good-for-nothing boy who stole your gold and your magic hen. No doubt he's hiding in the oven."

But Jack wasn't there, only several pork roasts cooking and sizzling. The Ogre's wife laughed. "How forgetful I am!" she said. "You smell the boy we had last night for dinner. He spattered all over the oven."

So the giant sat down to eat his breakfast, but every now and then he would mutter,

> "Fee-fi-fo-fum!
> I smell the blood of an Englishman.
> Be he live or be he dead,
> I'll grind his bones to make my bread."

And then he'd get up to search inside the cupboards and behind the doors, but luckily for Jack he never looked inside the copper pot.

When he had finished his meal of fourteen smoked salmon, fifty-five mutton chops, a small mountain of mush, and hot chocolate, of course, the Ogre called out, "Wife, bring me my golden harp!"

His wife placed a little harp before him on the table, then went upstairs to make the beds. The Ogre leaned back in his chair. "Sing!" he said. And the little harp began to play very sweetly, first one song, then another and another, until the Ogre fell fast asleep.

When the Ogre's snores sounded like a dozen roaring dragons, Jack knew it was safe to leave the copper pot. Silently he tiptoed to the table, grabbed the harp, and raced out the door. But before he'd even left the yard, the golden harp cried out, "Master, master!" and the Ogre awoke just in time to see Jack disappearing with his harp.

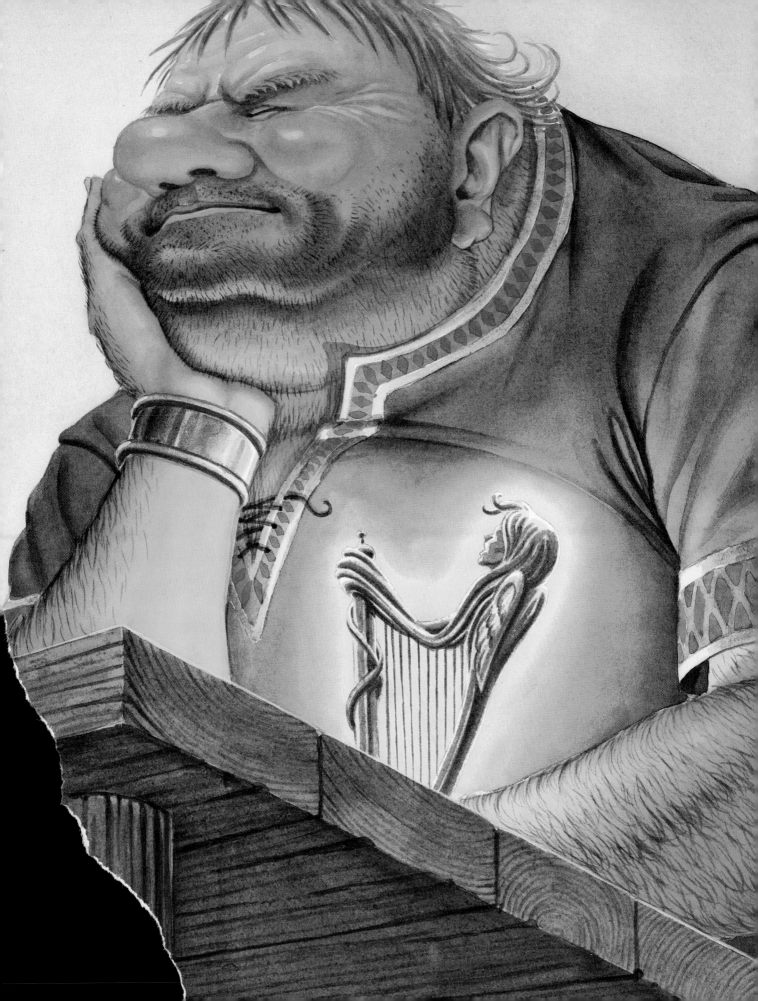

"This is the last straw!" the Ogre roared as he leaped to his feet. "I'll have you tonight for my dinner, boy!" And he ran out the door after Jack.

Jack ran like the wind and never stopped even once to look back over his shoulder, but he could hear the Ogre gaining on him. Closer and closer and closer, until Jack could feel hot Ogre breath on his back. By then he had reached the beanstalk. Jack leaped onto it and started down. He could see the Ogre up above, gingerly fingering the beanstalk, uncertain if it would hold him. This put Jack ahead again, and he climbed all the harder.

He was just beginning to feel safe when the little harp called out once more, "Master, master!" At that the Ogre made up his mind. Jack felt the beanstalk lurch and shudder, and knew that the Ogre was following him.

Down Jack climbed, faster and faster and faster. As he neared the bottom, he called to his mother, "Mother! Mother! Quick! Bring me an ax!" So when Jack jumped off the beanstalk, his mother was right there ready with the ax. Above them the Ogre's legs were just coming through the clouds.

Jack seized the ax and swung it as hard as he could into the beanstalk. A second blow and the beanstalk quivered. A third and Jack had chopped it clean in two. The Ogre roared one last time as he crashed to the ground, and the beanstalk came tumbling after.

Then Jack showed his mother the golden harp, which played more sweetly now than ever before. Hearing it, the little black hen tilted her head and cackled twice and laid a golden egg without even being asked. And after that Jack and his mother were never short of music, or of golden eggs, or of amazing stories to tell their friends about a rich Ogre's widow who lives above the clouds.